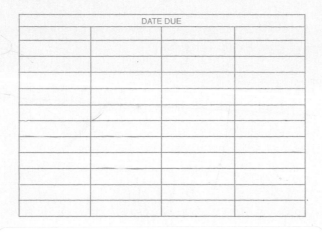

DATE DUE

For Lisa, the Brave
B. B.

To Sonny
K. M. D.

First edition 2010

Library of Congress Cataloging-in-Publication Data is available.
Library of Congress Catalog Card Number 2010007513
ISBN 978-0-7636-4101-6

10 11 12 13 14 15 16 LEO 10 9 8 7 6 5 4 3 2 1

Printed in Heshan, Guangdong, China

This book was typeset in New Baskerville.
The illustrations were done in watercolor, ink, and gouache.

Candlewick Press
99 Dover Street
Somerville, Massachusetts 02144

visit us at www.candlewick.com

A Bedtime for Bear

Bonny Becker

illustrated by

Kady MacDonald Denton

CANDLEWICK PRESS

Everything had to be just so for Bear's bedtime.

His glass of water had to sit on the exact right spot on his bed stand.

His favorite pillow must be nicely fluffed.

His nightcap needed to be snug.

Most of all, it had to be quiet—very, very quiet.

One evening, Bear heard a tap, tap, tapping on his front door.

When he opened the door, there stood Mouse, small and gray and bright-eyed.

He clasped a tiny suitcase in his paw.

"I am here to spend the night!" exclaimed Mouse with a happy wiggle of his whiskers.

"Surely we agreed on next Tuesday," protested Bear.

"No," said Mouse. "You most definitely said tonight."

"Oh," said Bear.

Bear had never had an overnight guest before. Guests could quite possibly mess things up and make noise, and Bear needed quiet, absolute quiet, at bedtime.

Even so, Bear and Mouse enjoyed an evening of checkers and warm cocoa, and soon it was time for bed.

"Remember, I must have absolute quiet," reminded Bear.

"Oh, indeed," said Mouse.

Bear set out his glass of water,

adjusted his nightcap,

fluffed his favorite pillow,

and climbed into bed. It was very, very quiet. He closed his eyes.

Bristle, bristle, bristle. Bear heard a noise. It was Mouse, brushing his teeth.

"Ahem!" Bear cleared his throat in a reminding sort of way.

"Most sorry," said Mouse.

Bear closed his eyes again.

"Humm, hum-pa-pummmmm," Mouse hummed while he put on his nightshirt.

"Pa-pummmmmm."

"Absolute quiet . . ." muttered Bear most patiently.

"Deepest apologies," said Mouse.

Creak, squeak, rattle went Mouse's bed as he hopped in.

Bear jammed his pillow over his ears, gritted his teeth, and closed his eyes.

He was just about to drift off when . . .

"Good night, Bear," Mouse called softly.

 Bear tried to pretend he was asleep.

"Good night," Mouse called a little louder.

"My ears are highly sensitive," cried Bear.

"Really? How interesting," Mouse said.

"Can you hear this?" Mouse mumbled into his pillow.

"Yes!"

"Amazing. How about this?"

Mouse said from under his pillow.

"Quiet!"

Mouse slipped under his blankets, crawled to the bottom of his bed, and whispered.

"Can you hear—"

"Silence!" Bear roared.

Mouse slid from his bed, went into the closet, and said in the tiniest possible voice into the farthest, darkest, teeniest possible corner of the closet, "Surely, you can't—"

"Will this torment never cease!" wailed Bear.

"Sorry, Bear. Good night, Bear," whispered Mouse, tiptoeing back
into bed as quiet as a . . . well, you know.

Bear fluffed his favorite pillow, adjusted his nightcap, and waited.

But there was no more sound from Mouse. At last it was quiet.

Very, very quiet.

Bear heard a shuffling sound. "Mouse, is that you?"

No answer.

Bear heard a crick, crick, crick on the floorboards.

"I know it's you."

No answer.

"You can't fool me," Bear growled, but he didn't sound very certain.

Bear heard a low moaning noise.

"Mouse?"

Silence.

Bear was sure something rustled on the floor.

"MOUSE!" he cried. "Wake up!"

Mouse stumbled out of bed, small and gray and sleepy-eyed.

"What is it?"

But Bear couldn't see any rustly, moany sort of thing in his room.

His room looked quite like it always looked.

"Nothing," lied Bear, still clutching his blanket to his chin.

"I must have been talking in my sleep."

Bear chuckled. But it was rather quavery.

"Ahhhh," said Mouse with a glance at Bear.

"Could I peek under your bed?" asked Mouse. "Sometimes
 I like to check for . . . things, you know."

"Well, if you insist," said Bear.

"Nothing," said Mouse from under the bed.

"You'll want to check behind the curtains,
 I suppose," Bear said.

"All clear," declared Mouse a moment later.

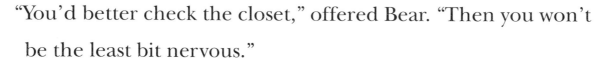

"You'd better check the closet," offered Bear. "Then you won't be the least bit nervous."

Mouse came out of the closet, dusting his paws.

"Not a thing. Thank you, Bear. Good night."

"Wait!" said Bear.

"You'll want a bedtime story, I expect," said Bear. "For your nerves."

"For my nerves?" said Mouse. "Oh, indeed. I'm quite shaken."

Then with an eager flick of his tail, he settled on Bear's favorite pillow.

And Bear told him all about the adventures of the Brave Strong Bear and the Very Frightened Little Mouse.

Soon Bear began to yawn.

Mouse yawned, too.

"Good night, Bear," said Mouse.

"Good night, Mouuuuzzzz," Bear mumbled.

Then Bear began to snore . . . LOUDLY.

But Mouse just smiled.

And soon Mouse and Bear were fast asleep.

Shhhhhhhhh . . .